EARTH DAY

Let's Meet

THE EARTH KIDS

Earth Kids care about Planet Earth.

Earth Kids are Earth Heroes!

by Barbara deRubertis
Illustrated by Thomas Sperling

The Kane Press
New York

ISBN 0-7915-1946-5

10 9 8 7 6 5 4 3 2 1

Planet Earth is in trouble!

People have not been taking care of this planet as they should. They have caused serious problems for Earth. It is time for kids like us to help.

We can begin by celebrating Earth Day.

Earth Day is April 22. This special holiday reminds us to take better care of our planet.

As we celebrate, we can learn about the air, water, land, plants, animals, and people on Earth. We can think of ways to solve the problems people have caused. Then we can work together to make Earth a healthier place.

There are two steps we must take in caring for our planet. The first step is to STOP doing things that harm Earth. The second step is to START doing things that help.

We can be Earth Kids!
We can learn how
to stop harming Earth
and start helping now!

Earth Kids care about Planet Earth.
Earth Kids are Earth Heroes!

Every time we take a breath, we use the air around us. We need the oxygen in air to stay alive.

Sometimes, the air gets so dirty with pollution, it makes us sick. It can also make plants and animals sick.

What can Earth Kids do?

We can STOP asking for unnecessary rides in a car. Every time a car starts, it adds to air pollution.

We can START walking, riding bikes, or using public transportation. In this way, we can help reduce air pollution on Planet Earth.

If the air that I breathe is polluted with smoke, it makes my lungs sick and I sputter and choke!

Smoke also pollutes the air we breathe. Sometimes, wood smoke from fireplaces forms an ugly haze in the air.

But some of the worst smoke is caused by people smoking tobacco. It is not only unpleasant, it is dangerous to our health!

By never *beginning* to smoke, we can
STOP the problems that smoking causes.

In a nice way, we can START asking adults
we know to stop smoking around us.
We can explain that we want them to stop
smoking because we care about *them*, too.

9

Water is a precious part of Planet Earth.
Oceans, lakes, rivers, and streams are
home to many plants and animals.
All living things on land also must have
water to survive.

But people are not always careful. When
they pollute water and shores, they cause
big problems for living things.

The birds at this beach
are all a-twitter!
Just look at this
disgusting litter!

We can STOP throwing trash into the water or onto the shore when we go fishing, swimming, or boating.

We can START protecting the water by collecting *all* our trash and disposing of it properly.

Even a rubber
duck can see
this kid is wasteful
as can be!

In many places on Earth, there is a
shortage of water. Some places have very
little water at all. Other places would have
enough water if people didn't waste it.

We can STOP wasting water when we
bathe, shower,
or brush our teeth.

We can START using
less water for baths.
We can take quick
showers. And we can
turn off the water
while we brush our teeth.

The land on Earth fills us with wonder.
High mountains. Deep canyons.
Rolling hills. Flat plains. The surface of the
land is shaped in many interesting ways.

Below the surface, the land is just as
wonderful. The rocks, minerals, and oil
found there are very useful.

But people are wasting some of these
precious resources. They are being used
up too quickly.

To help, we can STOP buying lots of metal or plastic toys, breaking them, and throwing them away.

We can START choosing and using toys carefully. We can recycle toys we no longer want by giving them away.

Oil and coal taken from the land are often used as fuel to make energy. Much of this energy is then used for lighting, heating, and cooling our homes and schools. Appliances such as refrigerators and TV sets also use energy.

The fridge is open
while a kid just stares.
The TV's on,
but no one cares.

The back door's open,
and the heater's red hot.
Are these Earth Kids?
No, they're NOT!

But the supply of oil and coal on Earth is limited. So it is important for people to use energy wisely. What can Earth Kids do to conserve energy?

We can STOP wasting energy at home and at school.

We can START turning off the lights when we leave a room. We can turn on the TV set *only* when there is a special program we want to watch. And we can put on a sweater instead of turning up the heat.

Trees are some of the most valuable plants on Earth. They give oxygen to the air. They provide food and homes for animals and people. Their fallen leaves enrich the soil. And trees provide protection from sun and wind.

Cutting down too many trees causes serious problems on Earth. How can we help?

We can STOP wasting paper, which is made from trees.

We can START making good use of *every* sheet of paper. We can make note pads from paper that has been used only on one side. We can recycle newspapers. And we can buy products that are made from recycled paper.

Plants provide most of the foods we need for good health. Grains, vegetables, and fruits all come from plants.

Artificial coloring and artificial flavor, lots of sugar, salt, and fat are here for me to savor!

But is that stuff all good for you? Somehow, I think it's not! A kind of food that's *bad* for you is what I think you've got!

In many places on Earth, people do not have enough food. It is sad to think that the food some people throw away each day would be enough to feed a hungry person.

We can STOP wasting food!

We can START being responsible about food. First, we can choose foods that are good for us. Second, we can take only as much food as we need. Third, we can eat what we take.

Animals are such an interesting part of Planet Earth! We know that each animal is an important link in the chain of life.

MANATEE
(U.S.)

CRAYFISH
(U.S.)

KEY DEER
(U.S.)

ANIMALS

TOOTH CAVE SPIDER
(U.S.)

GIANT PANDA
(CHINA)

SPIDER MONKEY
(CENTRAL AMERICA)

WHOOPING
CRANE
(U.S.)

DEVIL'S HOLE PUPFISH
(U.S.)

But people have not always been friends to Earth's animals. They have killed large numbers of some animals. They have destroyed the homes and food supplies of others. Some of these animals are now "endangered species."

Earth Kids can help protect Earth's wildlife.

We can STOP teasing animals or hurting them needlessly.

PEREGRINE FALCON
(U.S.)

LEOPARD
(AFRICA/ASIA)

CAROLINA NORTHERN
FLYING SQUIRREL
(U.S.)

ATLANTIC
LOGGERHEAD TURTLE
(U.S.)

CROCODILE
(U.S.)

NORTHERN
WHITE RHINOCEROS
(AFRICA)

SAN FRANCISCO
GARTER SNAKE
(U.S.)

We can START learning about animals we don't understand or appreciate. Even animals like spiders, bats, and snakes are valuable. They help control pests that feed on crops. And they are an important part of life on Planet Earth.

Many people enjoy having animals as pets. But some people do not care for their pets properly. Their pets are not given the water, food, or shots they need to stay healthy. Also, some people allow their pets to cause problems for other animals and for people.

Earth Kids can help!

We can STOP neglecting pets and allowing them to cause problems for others.

We can START giving pets good care every day. We can train them to have good manners. And we can clean up after them when they make a mess.

People are an important part of Planet Earth. The choices we make can either harm or help the planet. In order to make smart choices, we must understand how all the parts of Earth work together.

We can do this by studying science and math.

We can STOP letting our minds and bodies develop lazy habits.

We can START studying science, math, and other subjects with enthusiasm. With the knowledge we gain, we can make good decisions for Planet Earth—and for ourselves.

People also make serious problems for other *people*. When they argue and fight, they hurt others and they hurt themselves. Instead of solving problems, they usually cause more problems.

What can Earth Kids do?

We can STOP arguing and fighting with others.

We can START making peace by making friends. We can learn to settle disagreements in peaceful ways. We can learn to cooperate and solve problems together. By doing these things, we can make Planet Earth a better place for *everyone*.

We know that Planet Earth has *many* problems. We have talked about only a few of the ways Earth Kids can help.

Glass and plastic, steel and tin. Each goes in a separate bin.

Aluminum, newspaper, too. Recycling is the thing to do!

By starting with little things we can do every day, we develop Earth-wise habits. We can also ask our family and friends to help. In this way, we will show others that we care about the future of Planet Earth.

There are some problems facing Planet Earth that are very complicated. We might think we can't do anything about them right now.

But just *learning* about the problems is an important first step. We can look and listen. We can read and think. We can ask questions and search for answers. Then we will be ready to tackle these problems in the future.

Earth Day celebrations are spreading around the world. It is one holiday we can share with all people, everywhere. Although April 22 is the official date for Earth Day, we can practice being Earth-wise *every* day.

We can be Earth Kids!
We can learn how
to stop harming Earth
and start helping now!